ROMEO'S
BIG BOOK OF
CLEVER IDEAS

ALAIN GRÉE

Button
BOOKS

Today is an exciting day for Romeo. He is going camping! He gets up extra early to pack.

"What will I need?" Romeo asks himself. "One collar for the beach and another for going out, something to read, a camping stove, flippers, plenty of dog food…"

Romeo ends up packing so much into his huge suitcase that he has to sit on top of it to get it closed. Finally, it snaps shut. He grabs the case's handle, but…

…why is it sticking to the floor?

Romeo pulls with all his strength but the case doesn't budge. Oh no! It's too heavy with everything he's packed!

Romeo doesn't want to leave anything behind. He'll just have to find a clever way to get his massive suitcase to the campsite.

"Books are full of clever ideas," he says to himself, and rushes off to the library. In a big book of clever ideas, Romeo finds a picture of a horse and cart. "That's just what I need," he thinks.

With a couple of brooms and the wheels from an old pushchair, Romeo turns his heavy case into a cart, just like the one in the book. Surely this will work?

He straps himself to the cart and… one, two, three – *heave!*

But, oh no!

Romeo may be strong but the old wheels are not. The suitcase is far too heavy for them and they collapse under its weight.

He'll just have to think of something else.

7

In his big book of clever ideas, Romeo spots a car – a much better idea! He finds a pair of old-fashioned roller skates and sits the case on top of them then climbs on board. It seems to work well. The suitcase and Romeo roll forwards.

But…

…they are on a steep hill so the case moves quickly but cannot stop. Romeo had forgotten that cars have brakes! He rolls faster and faster, until…

CRASH!

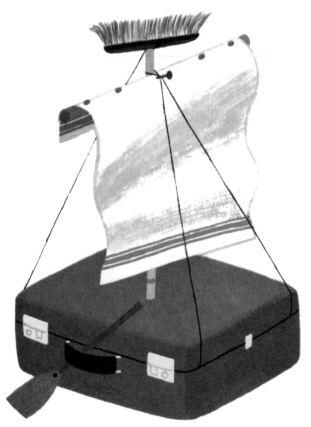

He'll just have to think of something else.

"Perhaps a boat would work?" thinks Romeo, looking in his book again. With a broom for a mast and a tea towel for a sail, he could float to the campsite.

But…

…the water is far away and the heavy suitcase can't float on land.

Perhaps it *could* float in the air? Like the hot-air balloon he sees in the book?

He ties a big bunch of helium-filled balloons to the case's handle. It floats up into the air with Romeo clinging on.

But…

…the balloon suitcase is soon out of control and heading dangerously close towards some overhead electric wires!

11

He'll just have to think of something else.

Romeo reads in his book that after hot-air balloons, inventors came up with the aeroplane. That should be a much safer way of getting to the campsite.

He uses bits of wood to make the wings and tail for his own aero-case invention. With two small wheels underneath and an electric fan on top for a propeller, Romeo is all set to go.

He switches it on. The propeller starts to turn and the plane trundles forward.

But...

...the suitcase is too heavy for the little electric fan to get it off the ground. He'll need to find something with much more power.

Turning the page, Romeo sees a picture of a jet plane. Now, they are much more powerful! But, how can he make his own?

He straps on an old vacuum cleaner for the engine and recycles the wooden wings from his first plane. He's ready to take off.

But…

…it just sucks in grass and twigs and mud! Poor Romeo.

He'll just have to think of something else.

14

15

"What is the *most* powerful vehicle in the world?" Romeo asks himself, and turns back to the book. Of course, a rocket! It has enough power to whoosh people into space!

He sets about making a rocket that looks just like the one in the book. He uses some wood for the wings and sticks a funnel on top for the nose. But the most important thing will be the rocket's power. He can't scrimp there.

Romeo gets some fireworks – the biggest, most powerful rockets he can find – and ties them firmly to the suitcase.

What could possibly go wrong?

Time for the all-important countdown. Romeo checks his watch. He strikes a match. Three, two, one…

17

BANG!

That was a *terrible* idea, and an extremely dangerous one!

When the smoke finally clears, Romeo sits down on the suitcase, which hasn't budged a bit and is now slightly scorched from the explosion.

He feels really sad. He was so looking forward to his camping trip, and now it seems he'll have to stay at home after all.

"I may as well start unpacking, then," he thinks, and starts to take everything back out of the suitcase. The dog food, the flippers, the camping stove…

When the case is finally empty, Romeo suddenly has one more bright idea.

19

20

It turns out the suitcase is so big he can shelter underneath it, just like a tent!

Who needs a campsite when you can pitch a suitcase in your own back garden?

Happy holiday, Romeo!

First published 2017 by Button Books, an imprint of Guild of Master Craftsman Publications Ltd, Castle Place,
166 High Street, Lewes, East Sussex BN7 1XU. Text © GMC Publications Ltd, 2017. Copyright in the Work
© GMC Publications Ltd, 2017. Illustrations © 2017 A.G. & RicoBel. ISBN 978 1 90898 598 9
Publisher: Jonathan Bailey; Production Manager: Jim Bulley; Senior Project Editor: Dominique Page;
Managing Art Editor: Gilda Pacitti; Colour origination by GMC Reprographics; Printed and bound in China.

**Button
Books**